# TINA SEARCHES FOR HER DREAM

*Nancy Ganz*

*Illustrated by Michelle Baron*

LUMIERE PUBLISHING

NEWTON, MA

LUMIERE PUBLISHING

Newton, MA

Cover design and Illustrations: Michelle Baron
*www.michellebaron.com*

Creative Consultant: Sara Ganz
Text design: Deanna Agresti
*www.deannaagresti.com*

ISBN 978-0-9993772-6-0

Library of Congress Control Number: 2019905804

It is important for children to see themselves reflected in the stories
they read. Therefore, we published three versions of Tina,
featuring diverse heroines

Thank you for purchasing this book through the publisher
and approved outlets. You can reach the author at:
*www.thenurtureguide.com*
@@thenurtureguide

Project coordination by Jenkins Group, Inc.
*www.BookPublishing.com*

Printed in Korea by Pacom Korea, Inc., First Printing, October 2020, #34917.1-D7
24 23 22 21 20 • 5 4 3 2 1

# arabasque
*(erə'besk)*

# développé
*(də,velə'pā)*

# jeté
*(zhə'tā)*

# pirouette
*(pirə,wet)*

## BALLET TERMS
*Pronunciation Key*

# plié
*(plē'ā)*

# relevé
*(relə'vā)*

# rond de jambe
*(rän də'zhämb)*

# sauté
*(sō'tā,sô'tā)*

How can it be
that a girl such as me
can't *dance* like the others
with a *dancer* as a Mother?

I practice and practice
till my legs *shake* and *shudder*...
but mine don't bend or stretch,
turn out, point or flutter.

Day
after
day,

plié, relevé,
pirouette, ronde de jambe,
arabesque, développé.

My friends dance with ease;

but for me it's a struggle.

With no boun<sup>c</sup>e
or boing,
I just stumble
and tumble.

When the teacher shouts
*Jeté* and then *Sauté*,

the students jump and leap

like birds soaring away.

But not me as you see,

'Cause I'm bent at the knee.

My parents are watching out from the crowd.

I want to do well to make them both proud.

But peering behind me it is clear to see,

*That being a dancer just isn't for me.*

There must be a better dream out there for me.

I tried SOCCER…

and BASEBALL…

and BASKETBALL...

and CREW...

but not one felt like the
dream I was meant to pursue.

Then one day I saw a girl on a horse trotting by,
and I thought to myself,
"Why not *give it a try*?"

I slipped my leg over top,
onto the horse I did glide.
And my bowed legs fit snugly
on the left and right side.

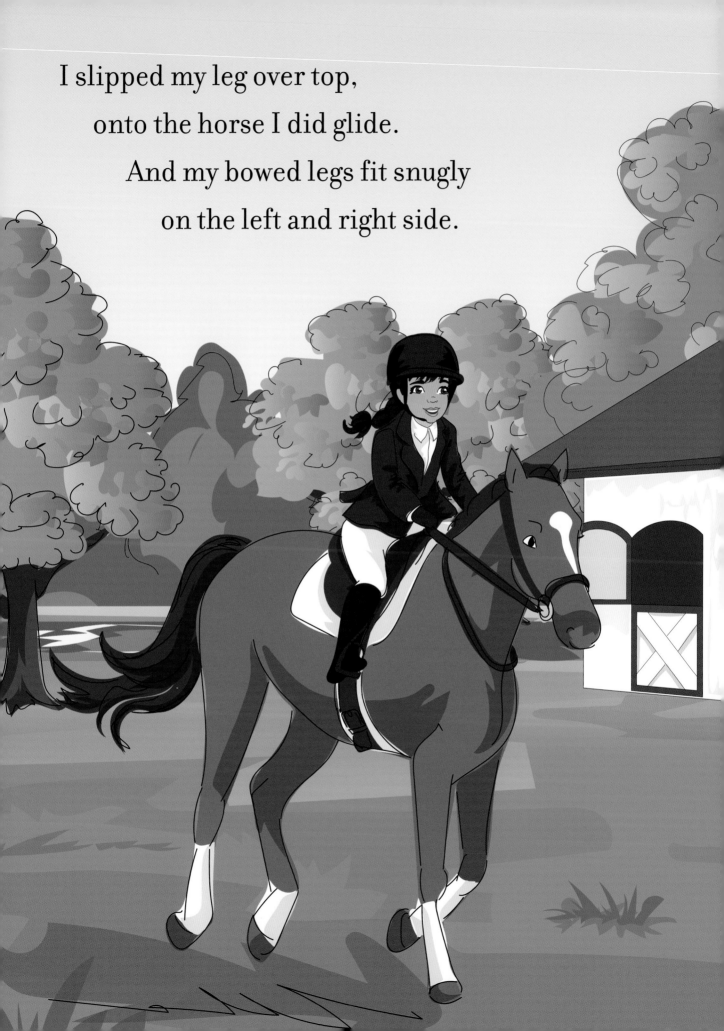

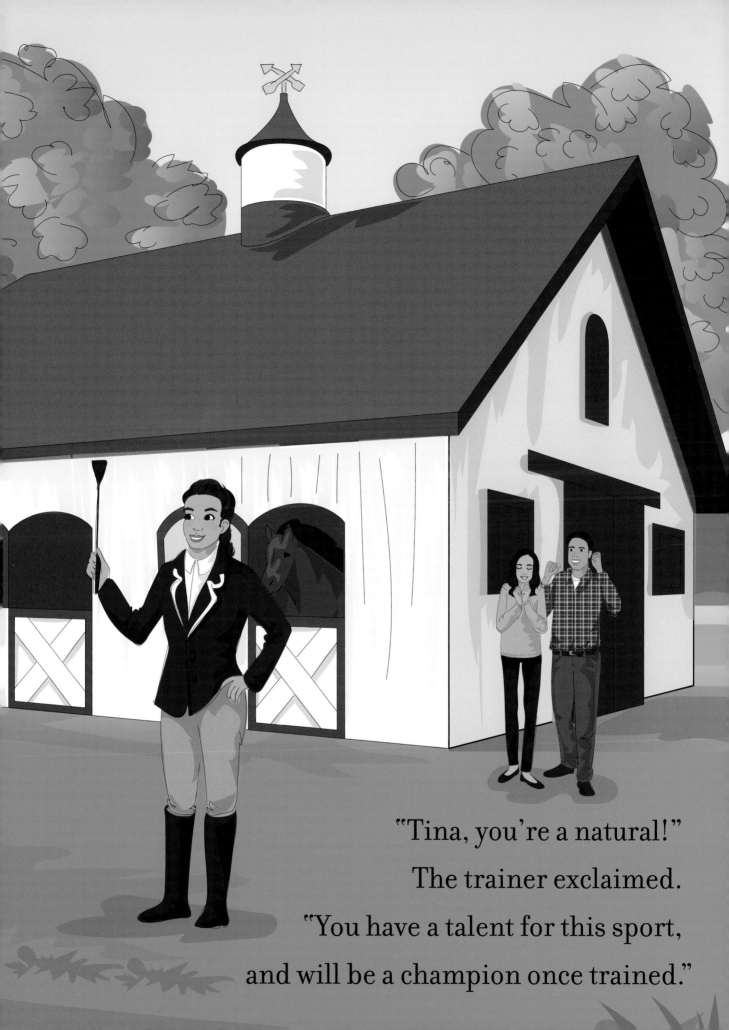

"Tina, you're a natural!"
The trainer exclaimed.
"You have a talent for this sport,
and will be a champion once trained."

The trainer called out waving her crop,

*"Keep going, keep going, keep going, don't stop."*

I flew over logs, then hurdles, then gates.

It wasn't long till I collected blue ribbons in eights.

My friends all came and cheered
with my joy on full display.

For on top of my horse,
I could *Jump, Leap and Jeté.*

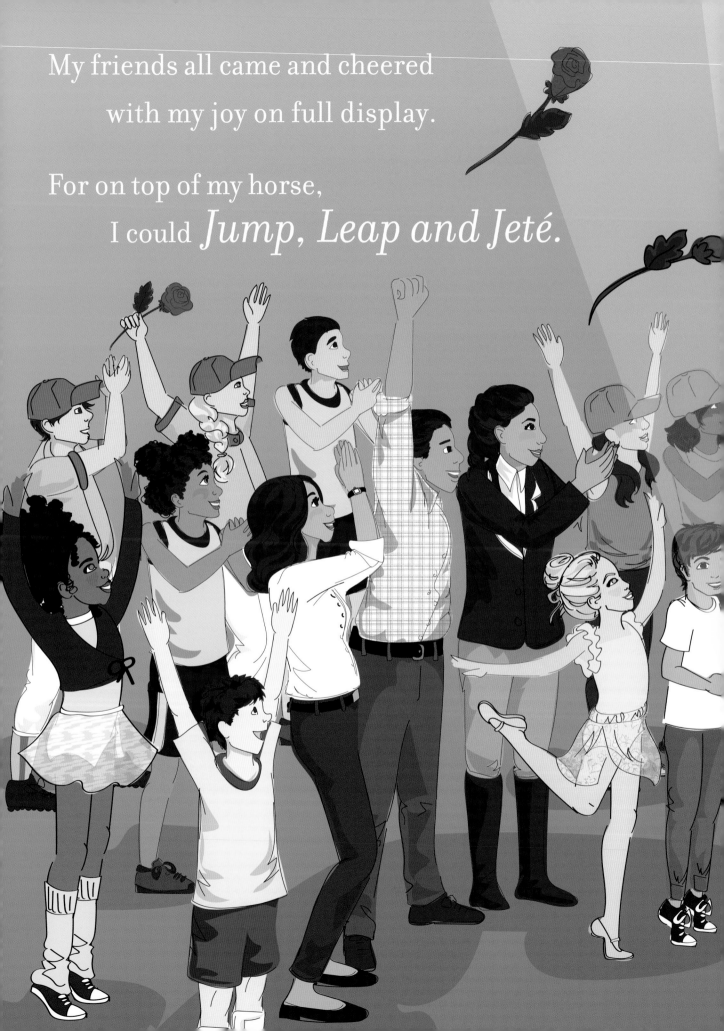

Find your

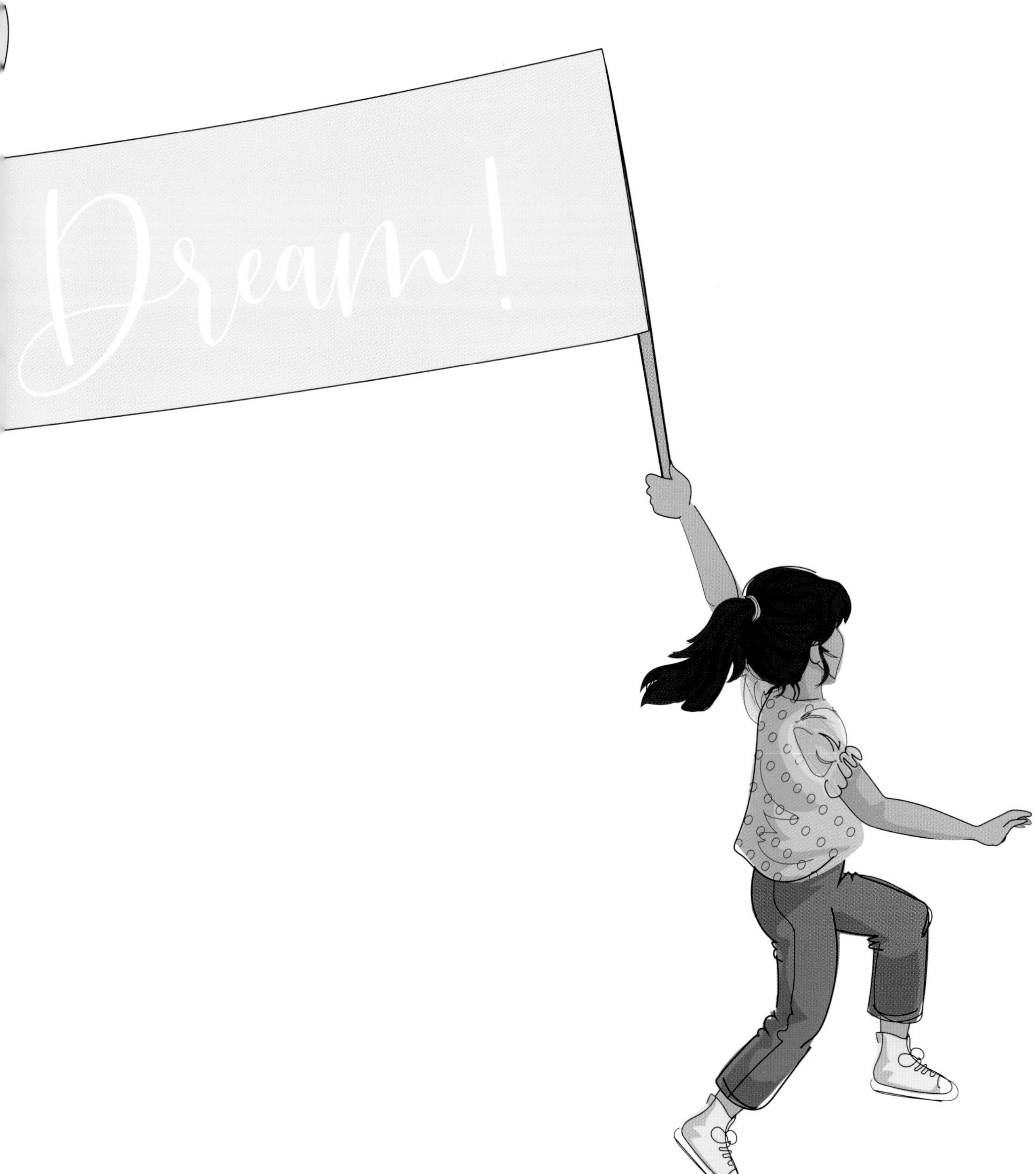
Dream!

DEDICATED TO YOU
*and your*
COURAGE TO DREAM.